Court & Dagger

and other tales from Exmoor

written and illustrated by

Chris Gladstone

Everything in this publication is a work of fiction. Many of the places mentioned are real but all the names, characters and incidents in this book are the product of the author's imagination and are entirely fictitious. Any resemblance to actual persons, living or dead, is purely coincidental.

Dedicated to
the people of Porlock

Contents

Court & Dagger

A ballad of Exmoor

I watch the glinting arc below where gentle waves caress the shore,
Whose ripples mirror timeless tales of secret loves, of pain and joy,
Of wicked deeds, of wicked men,
Of broken hearts and lovers' plights,
Of countless vivid vital lives that cling so briefly to this land
And to this wild and silent moor.

Exmoor Friday night

Shouting, bumping, laughing, spilling, trayful waiters spin,
Windows dripping, rock band thumping, heaving in the inn.
Landlord sweating, burgers wafting, empties piling high,
Real ale flowing, cheeks a'glowing; Exmoor Friday night.

In one corner, usual place, their evening scarce begun
Were four pub veterans, grey-haired all, just watching all the fun.
Bill ex-banker, Vince ex-copper, Fred The Forge ex-smith
And Bob The Box, ex-undertaker: Proper Jobs and crisps.

Near them, Dave and Pete The Prowl, with one eye on the girls;
Tourist talent, G&Ts, high heels and plastic pearls.
Then, from outside, the roar of quads despite the din within
And moments later, local lads plus girlfriends swaggered in.

With callous disregard for form, they barged their way up front,
Swearing at complaining souls, their usual bar-room stunt.
Across the room with mates and shots, young Sal, green-eyed, saw all;
Her sister with the leading lout – so handsome, dark and tall!

Vince grumbled, 'It's that Cal again, amazed that he's not barred.
He's nowt but trouble, always was, he should be on a charge.
He acts as if he owns the place, just like his felon dad.
No respect for anyone. Those Dagmers, always bad!

'Their nickname, Dagger, suits them well. They're dangerous and wild.'
'I know', said Fred, 'Not gentle folk, aggression's more their style.
They say that Cal's not right up there, just too much apple hooch,
The stuff that Mog brews on their farm, it turns the brain to mush.'

'Here, look,' said Bob, 'Up at the bar. I think Tone's having words.
They say Cal's on his final caution, soon be barred for good.'
'Young Laura there don't look too pleased,' Bill noted. 'Don't know why
That bright young girl goes out with Cal, there's better blokes nearby.'

The argy-bargy at the bar was soon and quietly quelled.
The old boys supped their precious pints; they'll be there 'til the bell.
Then, by their side, a man appeared, he tried to find some room.
A tallish stranger, golden tan, fair-haired and smartly groomed.

The boys had stacked their well-worn coats, a small stool underneath.
The stranger saw it, much relieved, and smiled with dazzling teeth.
'I don't suppose, kind gentlemen, that I could sit awhile?
I've travelled quite a distance here. I'm thirsty and real tired.'

They eyed him up and sized him up – American, no less.
Expensive shoes, a tailored shirt, the hallmarks of success.
'Of course,' said Bob, 'Please be our guest. This stool is sort-of free.
Long way from home and on your own. On holiday maybe?'

'Well, no,' he said, 'I'm on a quest, to find my ancient roots.
It's thought my folks came from these parts, were people of repute.'
'So what's your name?' Fred asked the man, 'I've lived here all my life.
I know the names of everyone, their cousins, dogs and wives.'

'The name's Bo Moore,' the stranger smiled, 'like Islay Scotch, I'm told.'
'A decent dram,' Fred nodded back, 'though Moores I do not know.'
Bo asked, 'A drink, kind gentlemen, for lending me this seat?'
'Thanks,' said Fred, 'I'll have a pint.' 'And me!' 'And me!' 'And me!'

As Bo stood at the crowded bar, Bob whispered to his chums,
'He looks well-heeled, game for a laugh. I think we'll have some fun.'
When Bo returned, sly Bob piped up, 'Here, Bo, you want to try
To solve this little trick I know? You guess it, then I'll buy.'

'Well, sure', said Bo. So Bob then placed a bottle upside down
And under it, a ten pound note, as Bo, uncertain, frowned.
'The trick,' said Bob, 'is to remove this note from where it lies.
The bottle though must not be touched or knocked onto its side.'

Bo pondered, supped and pondered more; how could this trick be done?
He knew these grinning local boys were simply having fun.
At last he said, 'Oh, damn it all!' and, grasping tight the ten,
He whisked the note from underneath. The bottle neatly fell.

Bob, laughing, set the trick once more. 'I'll show you, Bo. Nice try.'
He rolled the note which gently pushed the bottle to one side.
'Of course,' said Bo, 'I should have guessed. I owe you one, maybe?'
'Thanks,' said Bob, 'Another pint.' 'And me!' 'And me!' 'And me!'

***

Now Pete and Dave, not far away, had seen this little show.
'Do you remember,' Dave recalled, 'that business years ago,
Those outlaws Will and Peggy Rigg, the millions that they stole?
Were holed up in America, were never seen again.'

'I remember,' Pete replied. 'An interesting affair.'
'And I was thinking,' Dave went on, 'this Yankee over there,
I wonder if he was involved, he's searching for his "roots".
Seems well set up, got loads of cash, new shoes and flashy suit.'

'I doubt it, Dave. Nobody knows where they went with the stash.
Just disappeared without a trace with all that lovely cash.
The cops were here for weeks and grilled Peg's sister, Rosie Hay.
But all in vain, they got away. Good luck to them, I say.'

The crowd had thinned. Across the room, Pete spied a giggling group
Of tourist ladies, wine in hand, no wedding rings on view.
He smoothed his tash and checked his hair. 'I think I'll try my luck.'
He winked to Dave, 'Be good, old boy. Ta-ta and don't wait up!'

All peaceful on the farm

'How's your mum, Jack?' Spider asked as they leant on the gate.

Cooling air, high thin clouds, rosy sunset strands.
A vast expanse of endless sky, pins of stars beyond.
A peaceful eve at summer's end.

'Doing okay, thanks,' Jack replied, 'but still not smiling much.
Putting on her bravest face but I hear the sobs most nights.
Been hard for her, all her life, my mum's been through it all.
I wish that I could help her more. I wish that Dad was here.'

The gentlest breath of westward wind
Kissed leaves among the boughs.
Then silence o'er the rolling fields
Cut by a buzzard's cry.

'I hear,' said Spider, 'that, last night, Cal Dagmer was an arse,
Causing trouble in The Ship, himself and all his mates.'
'You're right' said Jack, 'I was there but didn't get involved.
No need to fuel this Dagmer feud, not publicly at least.'

'I'm with you, Jack, if you need help, you know I'm on your side.
Cal won't give up, still wants your farm, you've got to watch your back.'
'Thanks,' said Jack, 'I won't back down, I owe it to my dad.
Well, mostly to my grandfather. Do you recall the tale?

'My grandad, John Court, owned this farm, had worked here all his life.
He did some beating on the shoots, a true man of the moor.
On one such shoot, they tallied up the birds at close of play,
Found dozens missing, questions asked, was serious stuff back then.

'They found them in my grandad's shed though he was not to blame.
He knew Jake Dagmer put them there, to frame him for the crime.
He couldn't prove it. Slander sticks, then he was shunned by all.
They found him hanging in a wood, a proud man felled by shame.

'The Dagmers wanted my farm then, my father held them off.
He always was a peaceful man but I am not like him.
I don't forgive, I don't forget, the Dagmers are to blame
For what they did to my grandad, my family, my home.'

Wisps of mist cling to the springs,
The purple heather fades.
Ponies hug to distant hills,
A lonesome pheasant calls.

They gazed upon the lush green fields, the ones the Dagmers prized,
And dwelt upon the passing year, the coming harvest time.
The springtide lambs all doing well, fat rabbits near the wood.
Dogs are settled, walkers gone, all peaceful on the farm.

'I'm worried, though,' admitted Jack, 'I'm hitting thirty soon.
My mother says I need an heir, someone to run the farm.
She may be right – my duty lies to those who came before.
If Courts no longer own this place, the Dagmers will have won.'

'It's never easy,' Spider said, 'when working here so hard,
To find a girl, to find a love, and one who likes this life.'
'I know,' said Jack, 'they're all paired up, the only ones I like.
I had a love once as you know but she's with someone else.'

'I remember', Spider smiled. 'Laura Hay from school.
She's turned into a beauty now, dark hair and lovely eyes.'
'I saw her in the pub last night,' Jack said. 'She smiled at me.
But now she's with that Dagger sod. I think I've missed my chance.'

'Now listen, buddy,' Spider turned, 'enough of all this crap!
Cal's had his way for far too long, it's time for us to act.
This stupid feud, now Laura too, he's hitting where it hurts.
Let's let him know that we're still here and that we're fighting back!'

'You're right', smiled Jack, 'we won't sit back. Let's stir things up a bit.
Let's knock him down a peg or two, let's see what we can do.'
'Well,' Spider mused, 'I've had a thought. It's Carnival next week?
Let's teach that Cal a lasting lesson – epic, something Greek.'

Of loss, of life and love

The High Street buzzed, the crowds were out, in tee shirts, shorts and shades.
Cameras clicked, ice creams dripped, a cloudless summer day.
Gaudy bags, stuffed with wares from quirky boutique shops.
Cafes full, pubs all rammed, and tots with lollipops.

On the search for fresh green beans, potatoes and a pie,
Rosie strolled, her eldest daughter Laura by her side.
She watched the tourists bustling through this picture-postcard place
And pondered how the world had changed at such a rapid pace.

Born on a farm not far away, the place was quieter then.
A hard but simple working life with forthright, honest men.
Her folk were there in times of need, support throughout the vale.
Apart, of course, from her ex-spouse, but that's another tale.

The village now, though, prospered yet despite the changing times.
Its heart still strong, its soul intact, its people bold and fine.
Her family still lived around, her daughters still at home,
But soon enough they'll leave to find adventures of their own.

11

'Hi, Rosie!' from across the street, 'I thought I saw you there!'
A tall man, waving, beaming smile, a shock of snow-white hair.
He deftly dodged a caravan and skipped across the street.
'And Laura too! My favourite girls – an unexpected treat!'

'Give over, Colin,' Rosie smiled, 'Your charm won't work on us.
We haven't seen you for an age, you keeping well, old fool?'
'Oh, yes,' said Col, 'and having fun, it's great to be retired.
I'm painting more, it's coming on; a brand new camera too.'

'How lovely, Col. You do seem in a very cheerful mood.'
'Well, yes,' said Col, 'I bumped into a most delightful chap.
American, called Bo I think, quite witty for a Yank.
He's here to find his roots, he says, may be here for a while.'

A bit more chat then Col strode off and down a winding lane.
A tractor passed, its trailer shedding wisps of golden hay.
Backpacked walkers sauntered by; the antique shops were full.
Pavements trimmed with hanging pots, their flowers in full bloom.

'You're quiet this morning,' Rosie said. 'Is everything okay?
You hardly spoke to Uncle Col, you seem so far away.'
'I'm sorry, Mum,' her daughter said, 'just got things on my mind.'
'Job or boyfriend?' Rosie guessed, 'Is Cal being good and kind?'

'Well, yes…and no. He can be sweet but has this selfish side.
He treats me well but, I don't know, he sometimes can be mean.
I'm so confused, Mum, not too sure if I should stay or go.'
'Let's talk about it later, love, I'm sure we'll sort it out.'

A pair of horses cloppered by, admired by clicking phones.
Scents of coffee, baking bread and church grass freshly mown.
Butcher busy, art shops brimming, Exmoor souvenirs.
Neighbours milling, laughing, chatting, smiles and gentle cheer.

'Oh, look,' said Rose, 'across the road, there's Meg, that ghastly crone.
A bitter soul, she never smiles, just always scowls and moans.
Mother to that wicked Mog, the one who brews that hooch
And sells those 'herbal' cigarettes to kids, or so they say.'

'You're such a gossip,' Laura said. 'I'm sure they're not that bad.'
'You must avoid though, Laura dear, a smile from that old hag.
One smile from her, you'll turn to stone! But you'll be safe, I'm sure.
In all her days of living here she's never smiled before.'

'You're full of fancy,' Laura grinned, 'I feel more cheerful now.'
'I'm glad', said Mum. 'Let's keep it so, it's such a lovely day.'
Sparrows twittered, martins swooped, eager wagging dogs.
Flags and bunting flanked the street, a colourful array.

'The place looks great for Carnival,' said Mum, 'this Saturday.'
'Can't wait!' said Laura, 'Should be fun. Some friends are taking part,
Been working on their floats for weeks, they're really good this year.
Cal's entered too, he's on a horse, it's some Round Table theme.'

They wandered on and in and out, and chatted as they went,
With old friends, new friends, parish news, hearsay and new events.
While Laura shopped for tasty treats, her mother stood outside
And talked with Pat, old Fred's new wife and Rosie's new-found friend.

Mum and daughter ambled home, the shopping finally done,
And talked of loss, of life and love, how Fred had found his one.
His heart had broken years ago, since then he'd lived alone.
His girl had married someone else, the only love he'd known.

All until, a year ago, while at the Porlock Show,
He met the newly widowed Pat, just moved in up the road.
They fell in love ('It was so sweet!') and married right away.
All the village wished them well, a joyous wedding day.

'I'm glad,' said Rosie, 'Fred has found a loving, caring wife.
He's worked so hard and up 'til now has had a lonely life.
What I'm saying, Laura dear, is never lose your faith.
Whatever hardships we endure, true love will find a way.'

Cunning versus brawn

It was the day the aliens came.

They milled beside the dancing sheep,
Who mingled with the football team
And, next to them, a circus troupe
And stockinged men from Moulin Rouge.
Cops and robbers, bugs and clowns,
Famous stars from Tinsel Town,
Fox and geese and racing cars,
A pirate ship, a Western bar,
A wooden horse, the portly Krays
And Snow White who'd seen better days.

The car park filled with massing floats, a florid, festive scene.
Make-up on, adjusting masks, all honing their routines.
Colours, music, banter, cheer, an evening full of fun.
The sun shone bright for Carnival, it smiled on everyone.

Not long to go before the off; all was set, but then,
Around the corner came Cal's float – as usual, late again.
He made his entrance on a horse, in silvered knightly garb.
Behind him came, with helms and swords, a motley crew of guards.

A marshal came and checked his sheet. 'King Arthur, I presume?
The order's set but wait just there, I'm sure we'll find some room.'
Laura there with sister Sal who said, with breathless sigh,
'He looks so handsome on his horse!' Laura rolled her eyes.

Spider, Big Tom, Jack and Phil were standing by their float,
The Trojan Horse, on sturdy wheels, a highlight of the show.
Dressed as Greeks, it seemed as if the battle lines were drawn,
With vain King Arthur and his knights; cunning versus brawn.

Jack crept off and soon found James, a friend from long ago,
Who decided in which order all the floats would go.
Ex-army captain James disliked the tiresome Dagmer clan;
'Rude bunch, scoundrels, causing trouble any way they can'.

Jack outlined in quiet tones a trick that they would play,
'Just a harmless, special treat we've got for Cal today.
Just put Cal's horse behind our float and watch out for the fun.'
James smiled and winked and tapped his nose. 'Righty-ho, old chum!'

Jack returned to finalise their bold and shrewd idea.
'Here, boys,' he whispered, 'Gather round. We need a volunteer.
You know the plan, we need someone to get inside the horse.
There's not much room so someone small. I'm much too large, of course.'

Big Tom piped up, 'I'd love to, Jack, but I can't squeeze in there.
My lean physique is well disguised by too much chips and beer.
I've had a thought, though. Little Tom, you still up for the jape?
You're small enough, you won't get caught – we'll make sure of that.'

'Love to, Dad, it should be fun! Been practicing for days.'
So, shielded by the ancient Greeks, the plan got underway
As Little Tom climbed through the door and lay down in the horse,
Facing backwards, in position, on the cushioned floor.

They closed the door. 'Are you okay, Tom?' Jack asked quietly.
'You found the hole and got your shooter and your bag of peas?'
Tom confirmed so Jack went on, 'We're starting. Good luck, then!
It's show time soon so be prepared, I will tell you when.'

With blaring horns and hearty yells, flags waving in the sun,
The grand parade began to move, cheered on by everyone.
Dancing, spinning, laughing, twirling, decked with colours bright,
It snaked its way up through the street, a dazzling, sparkling sight.

Along the route, the crowds went wild, the show was in full swing.
So much movement, music, drums, the noise was deafening.
The queen upon the royal float dispensed her regal waves.
Excited kids were kept in line in case they misbehaved.

Of all the floats, the wooden horse was deemed the grandest one,
Much to jealous Cal's disdain, who wouldn't be outdone.
Behind the Greeks he pranced and jeered at Jack and Spider's boys,
Despite his slightly nervous horse (because of all the noise).

Tempted to unleash the ruse, Jack wouldn't take the bait.
He knew he had to bide his time, the prank was worth the wait.
His patience held and, as the floats came closer to the end,
He tapped the horse, gave Tom the nod, alerted all his friends.

Now, Little Tom, a wayward lad, was well known at his school.
His pea-shoot skills, fine-tuned in class, would now be put to use.
There was a hole, the horse's arse, behind the bushy tail.
Tom stuck his shooter slowly out and carefully took aim.

Cal's horse was only yards away; Tom checked his aim was true.
A big deep breath, a steady hand, he filled his lungs…and blew.
The pea shot out and hit the horse a tad above a knee.
It flinched a bit then settled back; nobody had seen.

Tom reloaded, aimed again and, with a mighty blow,
Sent the pea, as fast as light, unnoticed, whizzing home.
His finest shot, discreet and true; Cal didn't have a clue.
It struck the horse upon its chest…and then all hell broke loose.

With startled neigh, the horse reared up and capered to and fro.
The crowd all cheered, assuming just high spirits in the show.
Cal lost control, he grabbed the mane, then slipped and tumbled down.
He landed with a feeble yelp and broke his plastic crown.

His camera down, Col winked at Jack and gave him two thumbs up.
'You get that, pal?' Jack asked his friend. Col beamed, delighted. 'Yup!'

17

Her heavy golden ring

Though tatty, threadbare, blue, green, marked,
It was still her favourite chair.
Laura rested, lamb and gravy lingering,
While Rosie clattered cutlery next door.
Idly spinning the ancient globe,
Pondering distant lives and dreams,
And her hazy own.

Pigeons softly calling for love up on the thatch
And finding it so easily.
Dog fidgeting, wagging, pawing,
Kitchen scrap hopeful.
Cat twitching contently by the blackened hearth.
Mousey, rabbit, sparrow dreams.
If only life was that simple.

Floorboard creaking, side lamp dimmed, Rosie came back in.
Settling in her corner chair with usual heavy sigh.
She smiled at Laura. 'Okay, love?' Her daughter, silent, nodded.
Sal was out, to who knows where. A quiet evening in.

'It's lovely sometimes', Rosie said, 'to sit and have a chat.
Like we used to, 'fore your boyfriends, work and all of that.
Tell you what, I think I have some sloe gin still around.
My sister's favourite. Fancy some? A lovely little treat.'

'Love some, Mum, that would be nice. Your sloe gin is the best.'
A shadowed corner of the room, the antique wooden chest,
Now filled with bottles, all half-full, where Rosie, stooping, delved.
'Ah, here it is. A few years old but probably much improved.'

Laura sipped and closed her eyes. Pure nectar, smooth and dark.
The taste of home, of warmth, of love, long snow walks in the park.
'It's wonderful, Mum,' Laura said, 'it's one of your best years.
I bet Aunt Peggy would have loved to be with us right here.'

'You're not mistaken,' Rosie smiled, 'Peg always liked a tot.
Was well-known for her Friday nights and endless rounds of shots.'
'I've often wondered,' Laura asked, 'you ever hear from her?
I mean, no contact all this time? It's like she disappeared.'

'A postcard here, a letter there, but that stopped years ago.
I don't know where she is right now or whether she's alive.
Police stopped asking long ago, they pestered me so much.
My sister's smart – she went to ground and hasn't reappeared.'

'What really happened?' Laura asked, 'I know you know the truth.
I've heard the stories, people talk, it's quite a local myth.'
So Rosie sat back, sipped her gin, her eyes looked back in time
And told the tale, of cunning, greed, of gangsters, flight and crime.

***

Her sister, Peggy, married Will, a proper Jack-the-lad.
He worked in London, property, they had a Chelsea pad.
In the '90s, times were good, real fortunes to be made
For bright, ambitious, hungry boys in the investment trade.

Doing well until the day that Will was asked to front
A not-quite-legal city deal, a dodgy laundry stunt.
All in cash, twelve million, commission worth the while.
So Will agreed; he had the balls, ambition and the style.

Maybe too much, so they said; we know what happened next.
He vanished cleanly overnight, with all the cash and Peg.
They had a baby, 'lizabeth; they took her with them too.
A gangster bounty on their heads; world-wide interest grew.

The cops found out, then Interpol, a massive global hunt.
Despite the search and to this day, they're all still on the run.
Porlock legends, old folk tell of Will and Peggy Rigg,
Who grabbed the cash then disappeared like Exmoor morning mist.

***

'I wish I'd known her,' Laura said, 'she sounds a feisty sort.'
'Oh, yes,' said Rosie, 'that she was. No shrinking violet, her.
I've spent my life with lively types, just take your wayward dad.
I'm glad to see the back of him, the drunken, faithless sod.

'When Peggy left and you were small, things weren't so good round here.
The constant calls, the national press, John didn't take it well.
He took to drink and met that girl then, on a whim, eloped.
The best things that he left me with were you and baby Sal.'

Absent-minded, Laura stroked her heavy golden ring,
The one her father left for her before he had his fling.
Emblazoned with an ancient ship, it was all she had,
A poignant token from her past, a treasure from her dad.

'So, Laura love, I have to ask, are you still seeing Cal?
You said that things were not so good, that he was being mean.'
Laura paused and dropped her gaze as if away in thought,
Then slowly raised her troubled head and all came pouring out:

'A charmer, good-looking, of that there's no doubt,
To begin with I liked him, he treated me well.
But sometimes he's selfish, he can be so mean,
Insulting, provoking, annoying, just vile,
Mainly to others but sometimes to me.

As if he couldn't care,
As if I wasn't there.

One moment he's sweet and the next he's a fiend,
And violent sometimes, I've heard from his friends.
But not yet to me, Mum, don't worry your head.

21

'And getting possessive, it's becoming a pain.
He once mentioned marriage, that scared me no end.
He just wants a wife to continue the farm,
Not much bothered who, but it sure won't be me.
I mean, I want marriage, I'm twenty-six now,
But never that devil, I'd rather die first.
But what are the options? The boys round these parts
Just want to have fun and get pissed with their mates.
The good ones all gone or just hiding away.

I'm scared, Mum.
I want to leave, I have to leave,
But I'm scared to.'

Rosie took another sip as Laura wiped an eye.
The ageless tangle, lovers' knots, all promises and lies.
She'd seen it all, the twists and turns, confusion, sleepless nights.
Her daughter needed, most of all, her mother's wise advice.

'When I was young I was bewitched by dark and handsome men.
Mysterious, their bodies strong, a foolish young girl's dream.
But I soon learnt that looks deceive, that princes don't exist.
A loving heart and gentle soul will always win the day.

'So, Laura love, you must be strong, you know what you must do,
And don't despair 'cause somewhere, someone's waiting there for you.
So when Cal calls, don't call him back and see him less and less.
He'll soon get bored and hopefully will pester someone else.'

Laura smiled, 'I'll try it though I'd rather tell him straight,
But that may be too dangerous, I know what he can do.
He's raging still about that fall, you know, in Carnival.
His pride was hurt, he took it bad, you know how vain he is.

'I thought it was hilarious but dared not break a smile.
Pretended to be all concerned about his poor grazed hand.
He thinks it was a vicious prank and all Jack Court's idea
And if it was, remind me to buy Jack a pint of beer!'

'I heard that too,' her mother said, 'no accident, that fall.
Just village gossip, mostly false but also sometimes true.
Not many here stand up to Cal, the fame the Daggers have.
Except for Jack, he takes no crap; a strong, courageous man.'

'I've known him since we were at school – a solitary type.
I've always liked him but, since then, our paths just never crossed.
I saw him in the pub last week. He smiled and I smiled back.'
Rosie saw a twinkling eye and took another sip.

A new tale had begun

Clapping, cheering, drinking, jeers, the night was in full swing.
The two-man band, guitar and pipes, drew breath and had a swig.
The pub was packed this Friday night, these boys had drawn the crowds,
Old sea shanties, some laments and others fast and loud.

Between the songs, the bar filled up, the taps on constant flow,
As Bill and Vince, in usual place, just watched the to-and-fro.
A speaker hollered: 'Right, some more? We know you like this one.
Pirate Pat, a bawdy tale. Be sure to sing along!'

Ship Inn veterans Bill and Vince sat by the unlit fire,
With usual trick, a coat-clad stool in case a friend stopped by.
Pete was there with buxom friend, sweet nothings in her ear.
Always dapper, flash shirt on, his normal pulling gear.

'…and he ne'er loved owt but gold and slaughter,
'Til he saw the eyes of the captain's daughter'.

The crowd joined in, the tumult grew, then, pushing through the throng,
Bo appeared in jeans and shirt as if he now belonged.
He greeted Bill and Vince, now friends, and ordered them more pints
And sat down on the proffered stool, his lively eyes alight.

'…and he ne'er loved owt but gold and slaughter,
'Til he felt the waist of the captain's daughter'.

Chit-chat here and gossip there, the boys caught up on news
Of who's done what, to whom and why; Bo listened well, bemused.
They talked awhile of good guys, bad guys, normal village life,
And of the Court and Dagmer feud, the tale of constant strife.

News exhausted, Bo jumped in and, eager as a child,
Told them that his research trip was fun and so worthwhile.
Although he had to head back home in just a few more days,
He'd learnt so much about his roots and wished that he could stay.

Museum trips and library books, a hundred hours online,
Talking to the older folk; he'd had a splendid time.
Could be related to a lord (he'd seen it on a tomb)
And maybe to the Lovelaces who'd lived in Ashley Combe.

'I'm happy for you, Bo,' said Vince, 'I'm sure that you'll return.
There's so much history in these parts, a great deal more to learn.
We'll miss you, Bo. So, as you're here for just a few more days,
We'd like to give you, if we may, more memories of your stay.'

As they discussed the fun they'll have, across the crowded bar
Sat Laura with her best friend Sue, in candid heart-to-heart.
Current topic (yet again) was boyfriends, what they've done,
Who's been good and who's been bad, and all the pros and cons.

Sue was happy, Laura not, so Sue, as best friends do,
Plied Laura with white wine and shots, their trick for lifting moods.
Then came the giggles, smiles and hugs, the easy, careless chat
And Laura soon forgot her woes and thought instead of Jack.

'I don't know what I saw in Cal, a stupid dumb mistake.
There's better men than him out there, though God knows where they are.
But Sue, a secret, please don't tell, I might be getting pissed –
I think I fancy that Jack Court, I think he's rather fit!'

Sue sat back, full glass in hand. 'Hooray!' she said, 'At last!
I've known awhile, you can't fool me, although you fooled yourself.
You've always liked him, haven't you, you cautious little minx?
And Jack is handsome, in his way. I think you're turning pink!'

Laura smiled, a bit abashed yet glad her heart was known.
They chatted more and, one glass on, romantic seeds were sown.
'You've got to meet him,' Sue advised, 'and see what happens then
And...oh my God, he's in the pub, look, Laura, over there!'

Clapping, cheers then thanks and lull, another song was done.
Pat had toured the captain's daughter, battles had been won.
The band sat down and had a beer, their set had paused halfway,
When Jack looked up and caught Sue's eye which quickly turned away.

And Laura with her, Jack observed. His heart then missed a beat
When Laura turned and glanced his way, with eyes so dark and sweet.
Their gazes met, perhaps too long, coy smile upon her lips.
Quite mesmerised, he saw her blush and felt his stomach flip.

'Are you okay?' asked Ron, Jack's pal, who'd joined him for the night,
And then he saw where Jack's gaze fell and saw his eyes so bright.
'My, my,' he said, 'that's Laura Hay, I know you fancy her.
You've always liked the dark-haired ones, it's blondes that I prefer.'

Jolted from his reverie, Jack mumbled something back,
So Ron, who'd seen a golden chance, then tried a different tack.
'Sue is there and I like her, she's blonde, has gorgeous eyes.
They're on their own, let's talk to them, go over if you like?'

Jack, being nervous of this plan, sat tight and had more beer.
Across the room, Sue watched it all and had a bold idea.
'I think it's time to speed things on,' and beckoned to the lads.
'No, don't!' said Laura, blushing still, 'don't do it – are you mad?'

Some mild persuasion from his friend, then Jack agreed to go.
They squeezed in by the smiling girls and bought them more pinot.
Before too long, they'd all relaxed; Ron and Sue had fun.
Jack and Laura side by side. A new tale had begun.

Into the surging pool

A tranquil evening in the bay, calm sea and golden sky.
Down at the breach, the tide raced in, an hour until full high.
Balanced on the pebble ridge, they gathered there en masse,
Lines of zealous fishermen, all on the hunt for bass.

Col was strolling, taking shots, new camera, flashy lens.
Jack and Spider, rods in hand, were there with fishing friends.
Col came over. 'Any luck?' 'Not yet but maybe soon.
I've seen some move, the tide is huge, last night it was full moon.'

On Weir-ward side, stone's throw away, divided by the flow,
Were Mog and Baggy, friends of Cal; like him, enduring foes.
Despite a brief exchange of looks and quietly muttered words,
They left each other well alone, abuse and taunts unheard.

Out at sea, not far away, a small yacht drifted by,
On a line for Porlock Weir, to home while tide was high.
Jack and Spider watched it pass; Bob the Box's boat
And two companions by his side, enjoying being afloat.

'Hey, Col,' said Jack, 'who's that with Bob? They're wearing flowery hats.'
Col squinted hard. 'I think it's Rose and Fred's new lady, Pat.'
'Oh, right,' said Jack, 'It just seems odd, he likes to sail alone.
He told me that he likes the quiet, prefers it on his own.

'I thought that Rosie,' Jack went on, 'was not the sailing type.
I know that Fred enjoys a sail, don't know about his wife.'
'You're such a gossip, Jack,' smiled Col, 'I'm sure they're all just friends
Enjoying such a lovely day. I'd love to be out there!'

In the meantime, 'cross the breach and casting out their lines,
Mog and Baggy eyed their foes with mischief on their minds.
Then, as they watched, Jack's ten-foot rod bent hard into the flow,
They heard him call out, 'Got one, mate! A big 'un – see it go!'

The mighty fish pulled here and there. Then Baggy turned to Mog,
''Ere, mate,' he said, 'you know how Cal's been growling like a dog?
He's still pissed off about those two. Let's try to cheer him up.
I'll make Jack lose that fish he's caught. I think we'll have some fun.'

So Baggy, taking careful aim, cast out towards Jack's line,
Hoping that his lure would snag and lines would intertwine.
Sure enough, as Jack's line zipped, the fish still pulling hard,
He felt a separate sideways pull and cheering from afar.

Baggy smiled, 'I got him, Mog! My casting was spot-on.
I'll tighten up and, you'll see, that fish will soon be gone.'
He shouted fake apologies while smirking all the time,
As Jack in fury cursed and yelled, still holding fast the line.

'That bastard Baggy!' Spider cried, 'he aimed for you, I saw.'
The lines still stuck and both men heaved, a frenzied tug-of-war.
Jack was strong but Baggy too. The two men held their ground,
Both near the edge as high tide raced and pebbles tumbled down.

'That little sod! I'll not give up,' said Jack, still holding tight.
'Let me help you,' Spider said and came round on his right.
Both grasping firm the straining rod, they gave a mighty pull
And yanked poor Baggy off his feet into the surging pool.

A yelp, a splash, a frantic flap, he gasped, let go his rod.
He swiftly turned and struck for shore but currents were too strong.
They swept him out into the marsh, a quickly growing lake,
While friends on shore were panicking; his life might be at stake.

He kept his cool and kept afloat, the current pushed him on.
He checked for any shallow isles that he could 'light upon.
He saw one near and struck out hard, was finally aground.
Now helpless on a raised mudbank as water swirled around.

Jack and Spider watched all this as Jack reeled in his line.
The ten-pound bass was still attached, still fighting all this time.
Behind it, trailing, Baggy's rod and line and shiny lure.
'You get that, Col?' Jack asked his friend. 'Oh yes, Jack, to be sure!'

'We shouldn't leave him,' Spider said, 'although he's got no brains.
You never know, he might do something stupid yet again.'
'It's all okay, mate,' Jack replied, 'I've seen Mog on the phone.
Help will be here soon enough. Come on, let's get back home.'

They packed their gear and, full of cheer, strolled back along the shore.
The sunset glowed, the grasses stirred, the seagulls gently soared.
'Fancy tea, guys?' Jack enquired, 'we've had a fruitful spell –
Bass and chips and, Baggy, thanks, a nice new rod as well!'

A lawless brotherhood

Late September, Upshot Farm. Cal sat and sipped his tea.
Wheelchair-bound, his dad sat close, a rug across his knees.
In the corner, Baggy too, in blatant ugly mood.
All were silent, pondering this unremitting feud.

The silence broke. 'I'm pissed off, Cal! He made me look a prat.
We must do something, make some plan, something to get him back!'
'Quiet, Baggy,' Cal replied, 'I'm thinking, give me space.
We'll take reprisals, I agree, to put him in his place.

'We've got to be more cunning, though, more clever,' Cal went on.
'There's more to this than tit-for-tat, we need a masterplan.
I've talked to Dad; our prime concern's the future of the farm
And time is pressing, ain't it, Dad, we haven't got too long.'

The old man raised his wearied head towards his worried son.
They both knew that his time was short, his race would soon be run.
The accident that crushed his ribs would shortly take its toll
And leave young Cal, his mum long gone, in lonely sole control.

'I need a wife and family that will secure the farm.
I've set my sights on Laura Hay, she's beautiful and smart,
But lately she's been slightly off and has been seeing Jack.
Just friends, I think. Another ploy by Jack to get me back.'

His father fixed a steely eye on his erratic son.
He knew too well his temperament, what badness he had done.
'You treat her well?' the old man wheezed, 'you said she was the one.
You need her here to be your wife so, son, don't screw this up.'

'Don't worry, Dad, it's in the bag. I've always been a gent.
I know she likes me, told me so, at least to some extent,
And when we marry, there's a chance we'll end up better off.
The Hays, we know, may still be rich; that bank job long ago.'

'Don't be daft, son,' said his dad, 'I know that Rosie Hay.
She's never had that sort of cash, she lives a simple life.
All the money from that job just disappeared abroad.
I don't know where and don't much care, her sister took it all.'

'Well, cash or no, I'm still dead set on Laura as my wife
And if the money's still around, our future's more secure.
Our farm's been running at a loss these last few troubled years.
We need to turn the tide around, we need some more ideas.'

They all agreed that times were hard and something must be done
And soon, before the bailiffs came; they couldn't lose the farm.
Like shifty thieves, they huddled down, a lawless brotherhood,
And plotted how to get the girl and rid of Jack for good.

Now, Cal was sly and devil-smart, his instincts sharp and keen.
He must ensure the plot was tight and that his hands were clean.
His grandad's ruse that killed John Court, it worked so long ago.
Something like it – hit him hard! For Jack, a fatal blow.

As darkness fell, the plan was set. First, Cal would talk to Mog,
Dealer of assorted drugs who also brews the grog.
They'll need a bag of pure cocaine. As Mog brews on their farm,
Illegally, has done for years, they think he owes them one.

Then plant the coke on witless Jack and, publicly is best,
'Find' it on him, tell the cops, ensure a prompt arrest.
Laura, who despises drugs, will fall into Cal's arms.
They'll marry, have a stash of cash and maybe buy Jack's farm.

'You know,' mused Cal, 'of Laura's sister, Sal – she's always pissed?
Fancies me like mad, you know, and jealous of her sis.
I'll try to chat her up a bit and get to know her well.
If we can get her on our side, our intrigue cannot fail.'

His father swept his grey hair from his cold and cutting eyes.
'I trust you, son, to do what's best; my time is almost nigh.
Be careful, though, be bold, be strong and choose your allies well.
If you're not here to run the farm, you know we'll have to sell.'

'I am a Dagmer through and through, and born to fight,' hissed Cal.
'We pick our battles on our terms and lose, we never shall!'
The fighting talk, with jugs of hooch, continued through the night.
When morning came, all doubt had gone: the plot was watertight.

No lock and no alarm

In Vince's house in Bossington, a knock came at the door.
Vince opened it and, right on time, his cheerful pal Bo Moore.
'Come in, come in,' he ushered him, 'I'll get the kettle on.
The others won't be long, I'm sure, so make yourself at home.'

Before too long, the room was full, the other three were there:
Bill the banker, Fred The Forge and James ex-grenadier.
Teas were poured and biscuits passed, all settled in their chairs,
Then Vince stood up and took the floor. 'We all know why we're here.

'This agelong Court and Dagger feud is getting out of hand.
First, Cal was felled at Carnival, then Baggy nearly drowned.
We guess that Cal is raging mad, will soon want his revenge.
Our good friend Jack might need our help in light of what's gone on.

'We know that Cal's a vicious sod, will hurt Jack if he can.
Been also mean to Laura and we can't put up with that.
Before Cal has a chance to act, let's get our oar in first
And put him out of action soon! Now, let's discuss the plan.'

Puzzled, Bo felt honoured too, allowed to join their scheme.
Whatever plan they would devise, they'd make a fearless team.
'We might be old', they did admit, 'but we still have the skills
To run rings round that Dagmer clan, they're easy to outwit.'

37

They knew that Mog had always brewed that brandy on Cal's farm,
In an old shed by the stream, no lock and no alarm.
They'd creep up through the combe unseen and sabotage the still,
Then slip away as quiet as mice into the Exmoor hills.

The spearhead troops were captain James, a former army man,
And Vince, ex-copper, six foot two, still handy in a jam.
'And Bo,' said Vince, 'you have a role, a vital part to play.
We'd like you to distract the foe, make sure Cal's out the way.'

'It's common knowledge,' Vince went on, 'you're here to find your roots.
So what you do is, go see Cal, tell him you have some news.
Your research shows you may be kin, you have some Dagmer blood.
You're loaded and you'd like to start investing in his farm.

'We know their farm's not doing well so Cal, the greedy sod,
Will welcome you with open arms, so you ask for a tour.
Then, while you're busy looking round, away from Mog's shed, mind,
We'll creep up, do our naughty deed, and slip away like that!

'Cal has guard dogs, nasty things, so mind he locks them up.
Pretend you have a fear of dogs, he won't object to that.'
Bo considered for a while; sounds risky, also fun.
'Okay,' he said at last, 'I'm in. So when will this be done?'

'We thought tomorrow,' James replied, 'Strike as quick as poss.
Catch the blighter off his guard and show him who is boss.'
Bo enjoyed another cup, he felt he now belonged.
An Exmoor plan with Exmoor friends. How could it all go wrong?

***

Low dark clouds, a chilly breeze, perhaps a chance of rain.
A rushing stream, straight off the moor, cut through the rough terrain.
Bo dropped them off, equipment packed, once more they checked the times;
One hour until they'd reach the shed. The men began to climb.

Hidden well in mottled garb, they pushed through undergrowth.
A startled sheep, a pheasant's call, scratched hands and whispered oaths.
Vince and James pushed up the combe, sometimes they had to crawl.
Close to the shed, they hunkered down beside a waterfall.

In the farmyard, Cal, with dogs, was working all alone.
He saw a car come up the drive, a car he did not know.
A man inside, looked like that Yank, he'd seen him in The Ship,
Here to find his roots, he'd heard, no doubt a wasted trip.

Cal chained up the snarling dogs, then Bo got out the car.
He deftly smoothed his spotless coat and lit a fat cigar.
To all intents a wealthy man, Bo spun his fancy yarn.
Cal smelt the cash and took the bait. Now he could save the farm!

When Bo went on his guided tour, the dogs still chained up tight,
The steadfast heroes checked their watches – now the time was right.
Keeping low and vigilant, they crept up to the shed.
No-one there, the door unlocked; no talking, gentle tread.

The door pushed to, they found the still and Vince undid his sack.
They saw the vats of apple brandy, full and roughly stacked.
'You got that flask of laxative?' James whispered to his mate.
'Yup,' said Vince, 'Let's get this done then leave them to their fate.'

A few drops into every vat, the draught was potent stuff.
They didn't want to kill the sods so that should be enough.
On a table, just half-full, a vat plus half-full jug –
The Daggers' daily drinking place, a dozen dirty mugs.

When they were done, about to leave, Vince thought of all the ills
Done by the Dagmers o'er the years and that continued still.
A vat half-full – a flask half-full; to James, a wink and grin.
He muttered softly, 'Sod them all' and tipped the whole lot in.

James looked shocked but Vince just smiled. 'Don't worry, mate,' he said,
'They'll think Mog made a faulty batch, he'll get the blame instead.'
They checked outside, the only sound the gently tumbling stream.
All was clear so out they sneaked and slipped away unseen.

A wondrous land with wondrous friends

'Well done, Bo!' the old lads cried while raising frothy pints.
'A real success!' 'We had some fun!' 'To you, you did all right!'
Bo sat there among his friends, content, as pleased as Punch.
He loved their barmy company, they were a joyful bunch.

Their plan had worked just perfectly, Cal didn't have a clue.
Confined to bed, the grapevine said, a harmful, dodgy brew.
Cal blamed Mog ('I told you so'), they've had a falling out.
A nasty stink enfolds, they say, the moorland round about.

The boys exchanged a knowing glance. Bill, spokesman, turned to Bo,
'You've been a sport so we've got you a treat before you go.
You're only here for two more days so, if you may be free,
Tomorrow night we'll show you something tourists rarely see.'

Bo was perplexed so Bill went on, 'Bob here's an Exmoor man.
He's got a most amazing skill, he learnt it from his gran.
James and Vince are coming too. I've got a truck – I'll drive.
Don't be late and wrap up warm. We'll pick you up at five.'

***

Right on time, they picked up Bo and headed for the moor,
Bouncing down some muddy tracks, a proper Exmoor tour.
They stopped quite close to Dunkery and all got out the truck.
Bob gazed about and scanned the hills. 'Looks good, boys – we're in luck.'

41

Evening mist, a gold thread sky.
A blackbird flits, a swallow dives.
Bracken browned 'midst purpled ground.
A mossy gate and scarce a sound.

Bob led them all behind some gorse, then he explained to Bo,
'We're up here at this time of year to see a special show.
There's red deer in these Exmoor hills and now it's rutting time.
The antlers clash, the big boys scrap, the stags are in their prime.

'We have a sport this time of year and bolving is its name.
You imitate a roaring stag, it's quite a skilful game.
And if a stag returns your calls, you might just win a cup.
I've seen a big 'un over there; I'll show you how it's done.'

Bo, intrigued, saw Bob stand back then cough and stretch his arms.
He took some deep breaths, closed his eyes and stood there, very calm.
Bill nudged Vince and quietly whispered, 'This will be a laugh.
Bob has picked the perfect spot,' and Vince replied, 'Not half!'

Bob splayed his legs, hands to his mouth, a mighty breath he drew.
Then from him came, both long and loud, a most impressive 'Moo!'
A startled Bo – 'My God', he said, 'that sounded like a cow!'
'I know,' said Bob, 'it sounds like that. Right, Bo, it's your turn now.'

Bo took the pose and limbered up, the way that Bob had done.
Behind him, stifled giggles, winks, the boys enjoyed the fun.
Bo let go; a mighty 'Moo!' resounded 'cross the hills.
'Not bad,' said Bob, 'now try again. I see you have some skill.'

So Bo, now bolder, tried again then, much to his surprise,
They heard a deep and drawn-out 'Moo!', quite loud and quite close by.
Then, heavy snorts and rustling gorse, the crack of broken boughs,
A horned and shaggy head appeared – a nosy Highland cow.

Bob laughed. 'It worked!' The others too were laughing fit to burst.
Bo realised that he'd been had, then joined in with the mirth.
Bob smiled, 'I'm truly sorry, Bo, you're such a decent bloke.
I saw the cow, could not resist, we know you like a joke.'

The gentle cow had disappeared. Vince turned to Bob and said,
'Shall we give Bo his real treat, a proper bolve instead?'
So Bob prepared and loudly raised a deep and feral roar
That resonated though the hills, across the peaceful moor.

No reply, so Bob drew breath and had another go.
From far away, caught on a wisp, a roar came, deep and low.
With spy-glass out, they scanned the land and on a crag they saw
A massive stag with sixteen points, a monarch of the moor.

And with him, more than fifty hinds all lying in the fields.
A few young bucks grazed at the edge and tried to stay concealed.

Echo floated, then was gone.
Silence once again.
A merlin cried, a rabbit moved.
A perfect summer's end.

Bo was entranced; he never thought that he would see all this,
A wondrous land with wondrous friends that he would sorely miss.

***

They dropped him at his B&B; a tear ran down one cheek.
The times he'd spent here were the best, the most amazing weeks.
Great adventures, tales to tell, his new friends sure were fun.
They'd left him with their cheery waves and 'Bo, we'll miss you, chum!'

Justice Exmoor style

Mid-October, Thursday night, quite crowded in the inn.
Cold front coming, fire was on, a cosy mood within.
Skittles teams, both loud and large, assembled with their mates,
Beer and cider going down well. 'Here's Johnny, always late!'

Fred and Vince and Bill and Bob, in usual corner spot,
Sipping on their Proper Jobs. The fire was blazing hot.
Catching up on what's gone on, the banter flowing free,
Village gossip, latest news, what's done and what might be.

They raised a glass to 'good old Bo' who went home just last week.
'And did you hear of old Jake Dagmer? Passed away midweek.'
With voices low and worried brows, they knew he'd been quite ill,
But heard he'd died of natural causes, was on loads of pills.

Cal's been quiet, thank God, they said, but back upon his feet.
'Has not a clue about our jape; we'll have to stay discreet.'
'His dad now gone, Cal owns the farm, has much upon his plate.'
'I wonder if he'll now grow up, accept his new estate.'

'I hope he does', said Vince. 'I mean, this feud has got to end.
You see young Jack and Laura there? I think they're more than friends.
They're getting closer, so it seems, though I don't like to pry.
I told Jack what we did to Cal, in case things go awry.'

And sure enough, across the room, the couple sat alone,
Absorbed in loving company, euphoric on their own.
They gazed, enamoured and with hope, into each other's eyes.
The speed and passion of their love had caught them by surprise.

In the meantime, stood outside and hidden out of sight,
Cal was waiting in the dark, hood up and jaw set tight.
His dad had died, the Yank had gone, his future still at risk.
And Laura too, she favoured Jack; he thought he'd seen them kiss.

In warlike mood, Cal checked his coat; the heavy bag still there.
Then, from the doorway, Sal appeared and Cal gave her a glare.
'You're late,' he snarled. 'I've been out here ten minutes in the cold.
Where've you been, I said half-past! Just do as you were told!'

'I'm sorry, Cal, I was delayed,' Sal simpered, 'Please don't shout.
You know how chatty Amy gets, 'specially when we're out.'
'I don't care. Just do the job and quickly,' Cal replied.
'Here, take the bag. Now duck round here, we can't be seen outside.'

They quickly checked their simple plan: 'On your way to the loo,
Pretend to notice Laura there, go over, say hello.
You'll see Jack's coat up on the door, he always hangs it there.
Then, when you go, slip in the coke and then we'll have him snared.'

'When you return, say hi again and lean against Jack's coat.
Pretend to feel a bulky bag and joke about some dope.
Get it out and then look shocked, start shouting, make a scene.
Make sure everybody sees, then call for the police.'

'I'm nervous, Cal,' admitted Sal, 'What if it goes wrong?
She is my sister, after all, I don't know I'm that strong.'
'Don't worry, Sal, she won't find out, and Jack will soon be gone.
Then you and I can be together, and we'll have the farm.'

Sal smiled, 'Okay, I'll do my best, I know you're always right.
I'll see you later once it's done. Can I come round tonight?'
'Of course,' said Cal, 'just come on up and see me, it's a date.'
The cunning fox then disappeared and left Sal to her fate.

46

Sal returned and had more wine to quell her knotted nerves.
Jack and Laura still engrossed, distracted, she observed.
She braced herself, a big deep breath, rehearsed what she would do,
Then grabbed her handbag, took a swig and headed for the loo.

'Hi Laura, Jack, how's life?' smiled Sal, her back against the door.
Some brief chit-chat but they were too preoccupied, she saw.
She turned around and from her bag she took the bag of coke.
She kept her cool and, like a thief, she slipped it in Jack's coat.

Vince creased his brow; he'd seen Sal's chat but something's not quite right.
The way Sal moved, a worried glance, perhaps a hint of fright.
A copper's instinct, never lost; he pondered then stood up.
'Hey, Sal!' he called before she left, 'Just hold on there, my love.'

Sal turned and, like a rabbit caught, she froze with open eyes.
Vince soon was by her; Sal's face fell, a tear, a quivered sigh.
'I think,' said Vince, 'there's something wrong. I don't know what you've done.
Just tell us, please, 'cause as you know, we'll find out 'fore too long.'

Sal sniffed and knew the game was up, she had to dish the dirt:
'He made me do it, honestly! I knew it wouldn't work.'
When pressed, Sal caved, pulled out the bag and, very sheepishly,
Put it on the tabletop for all the world to see.

They all went silent, stunned and shocked; Sal bowed her head in shame.
Jack and Laura stared at her, then knew Cal was to blame.
She spilled the beans: get Jack sent down then Cal would buy his land
And marry Sal, his one true love – he was her perfect man!

'This is,' said Vince, 'an awful mess. Here, Jack, I want a word.'
They went outside; their quiet chat could not be overheard.
Vince asked what Jack would like to do, they ought to call the cops,
And Jack agreed: Cal would go down, at last the feud would stop.

But… wait a mo, another plan – Jack had a new idea.
'Don't tell the cops, not good for trade, we do things different here.
Instead, if Cal does one more wrong, we'll say, however small,
We'll tell the cops, get him locked up. We have him by the balls!'

'I like that plan,' smiled Vince, 'it's graceful – justice Exmoor style.
But Jack, you seem to be quite calm, you should be spitting fire?'
'I'm angry, Vince, and, other days, I'd spoil Cal for a fight,
But not tonight, I must stay cool, got something on my mind.'

A glance to Laura, love-struck eyes. 'I see, Jack – say no more.'
Vince winked at Jack and took the bag, 'Pretend you never saw.'
Sal had gone, chastised and shamed. Vince went back to his friends
And told them all the sorry tale, more drama yet again.

***

'I don't believe what just went on,' said Laura. 'What a git!
I don't blame Sal, she's so naïve. Cal's up to his old tricks.'
Alone again, they talked it through and soon had both calmed down,
Back to their smiles and loving talk, the closeness they had found.

Jack was nervous, not sure why, he'd known her since at school.
He'd loved her since the day she laughed and pushed him in the pool.
A silent hope, a heartbeat jump, a prayer to gods above,
He turned to her and took her hand and pledged undying love.

She watched him with her deep dark eyes, a smile upon her lips,
Saying nothing, holding tight and then a gentle kiss.
He stroked her hair and whispered softly, 'Will you marry me?'
She whispered back, 'Of course I will,' and kissed him lovingly.

***

'I think', said Fred, 'those lovers there are more than happy now.
If I'm not wrong, before too long, we might hear wedding vows.'
'We've known her since she was a pup; she's now grown up,' said Bill.
'We always have looked after her and, lads, we always will.'

'If this goes well,' continued Bill, 'and Laura marries Jack
And we decide to spill the beans, there'll be no turning back.'
'A risk,' said Fred, 'but Laura's smart and canny, I am sure.
Jack is sound and, with the cash, her future is secure.'

'A mighty shame, though,' Bill went on, 'that Cal's not in the clink.
But well done, lads, Phase One complete. Let have another drink.'
They supped their pints. Bill turned to Fred, 'So what about Phase Two?'
Fred paused for thought, a worried brow. He mumbled, 'Soon, Bill, soon.'

***

'Ahem!' said Vince, 'We have a snag,' and pointed to his hat,
Where, underneath, a certain bag of something duly sat.
They looked around and scratched their heads. So what were they to do?
Can't return it, cannot keep it, problems would ensue.

They all agreed the bag must go, it had to be destroyed,
But how? At sea, or scatter it, or drop it in a void?
Bob sighed and said, 'Oh sod it, lads,' and chucked it on the fire.

A mellow time was had by all, a most reposeful night.

A ragged shade across the deadly moor

A few weeks on, up on the moor, the shooting had begun.
City boys with spotless cars, new tweeds and shiny guns.
Splash the cash and sink the fizz, no-one was keeping score.
Accents clipped and sneering lips, a hundred birds or more.

A sheet of frost embraced the land, the wind was deadly cold.
Leaden clouds moved from the west, might snow soon, they were told.

Scarves wrapped tight,
The quiet walk down
The stony forest track.

Heavy breath clouds,
Dogs subdued,
Dark firs like stakes of jet.

Icy footprints, silvered webs,
Shadows through the trees.
A lonesome crow,
Soft crunch steps.
The silence of the dead.

All in place, long trails of dew across the crispy grass.
Muted banter, keeping warm, expectant, whisky flasks.
Some local lads, the favoured few, invited for the day.
A bit of sport then slap-up meal and let the rich boys pay.

51

Cal was there; he knew the crew, they sometimes used his woods.
He liked to shoot, to soothe his moods, was reckoned rather good.
With him, his trusty side-by-side – he'd make those pheasants dance!
And Sal, his loader for the day; she wanted one more chance.

Sal had told him everything, Jack's threat about the cops.
Cal bowed his head and promised Jack, for sure, the feud would stop.
He knew of the engagement plans, he knew that Jack had won.
He'd toe the line, he'd stay with Sal, he'd focus on the farm.

But underneath, Cal fumed and raged; how could they treat him so?
Embarrassed, threatened, Laura gone, in debt and savings low.
He was a Dagmer after all, they never lost a fight!
He had to think – there must be ways to save him from this plight.

The wind increased, the sky turned black, the snow began to fall.
Before too long, an icy storm had swept across the moor.
The fir trees tipped, the snow lay thick, the shooting had to stop.
The rich boys moaned then found their lifts and headed for the lodge.

A slushy track, a snowful ditch, two four-by-fours got stuck.
The boys all pushed and pulled and swore but 'Sorry lads, no luck'.
Cal stayed back to offer aid, Sal was with him too.
Someone called the nearest farm – 'Tractor needed, soon!'

It happened that Jack's farm was close, the nearest thereabout.
He quickly rigged up towing chains and had the cars pulled out.
With thanks and waves, the men drove off, all keen to get inside,
Leaving Jack and Laura there – she'd come out for the ride.

With freezing hands, she cuddled close. 'Let's get back to the farm.
I'll get the fire on, feed the dogs, then you can keep me warm.'
Jack held her close, smiled to himself, 'I'm such a lucky man.'
Then, from a tree, in swirls of snow, came Cal with gun in hand.

Tall and sombre, Cal stood still with Sal not far behind.
Stony faced and knuckles white and evil on his mind.
He'd seen them there, the warm embrace, the love he'd never know.
He felt the fire rise to his eyes and his fury grow.

Jack and Laura saw him there, defiant, silent, grim.
Open ground, just yards apart and light becoming dim.
Still no words, the men just stared. Jack knew he couldn't run.
Cal then smiled and licked his lips and slowly raised his gun.

Years of hatred, fighting, anger, insults, broken vows.
His blood was up, his time was now, his father would be proud.
The land was hid, the snow lay thick, a bitter winter storm,
But even so, Cal's gun felt good, the trigger strangely warm.

He took his aim; he couldn't miss, of that there was no doubt.
'No!' yelled Jack, 'Don't do it, Cal! Let's try to work this out!'
Too late, thought Cal and took a breath. Sal gasped and Laura shrieked.
'Goodbye, Jack', a final smirk… then something smashed his knee.

He buckled, slipped, and hit the ground,
Sal beside him, stick in hand.
She shouted loud and hit him more,
He yelled and grabbed her, swearing hard.
Getting up, gun still in hand,
She kicked him down with all her might.
Again he rose; Jack bearing down.
Cal, unbalanced, swung his gun.

The gun went off…
And Sal went down.

Cal scrambled up, now on his feet, and saw Sal lying there,
Twisted in a snow-filled ditch, eyes closed and bloodied hair.
He dropped his gun and ran from Jack, where to, he wasn't sure,
And disappeared, a ragged shade across the deadly moor.

Well disguised

Morning time at Rosie's house, the fire and kettle on.
Fred and Pat had visited and Laura was at home.
They talked of Sal, a lucky girl, in hospital and sore.
The pellets hit her shoulder, just a light wound, nothing more.

Cal was caught out on the moor, the dogs had tracked him down.
They found him in a quaking bog, they say he almost drowned.
Arrested for this latest crime and several sins before,
The Dagmers were restrained at last, no problem any more.

'So what about these wedding plans?' Fred and Pat both beamed,
And Laura smiled, 'Yes, Christmas time, it's always been my dream.
I mean, why wait when you're in love?' and Fred said, 'I agree.
Jack Court is such a fine young man and true love is the key.'

The doorbell rang and Bill came in, wide-eyed, in flustered state;
'Sheep on road. I'm sorry, all. I hope I'm not too late?'
Rosie smiled, 'It's okay, Bill, just sit down on that stool.
We wouldn't start without you here, you have a vital role.'

They all sat down and looked around, a tension in the air.
Rosie coughed and looked at Pat, then turned to Laura's chair.
'We have something to tell you, darling.' Laura looked confused.
'About the past, about your life. It's time you knew the truth.'

Looking nervous, Rosie paused, she had become quite pale.
She took a breath, composed herself and then began the tale.

**

Her sister, Peggy, married young to dashing wide-boy Will,
Enticed by diamonds, pearls and lights and normal city thrills.
They had a baby, blonde-haired Liz, she had her father's looks,
And then the scandal, then the flight, the millions that they took.

'You know this story, Laura love. However, there's a twist.
They knew the mob might track them down and also the police.
The search was on, a global hunt for man and wife and child,
But Peg and Will had tricked the world, deceived them all the while.

'For if they're caught, as they may be, the child would be alone.
Mum and dad in gaol or worse, Liz taken and rehomed.
They couldn't take their baby girl, too dangerous, you see,
And so they left her, secretly, with relatives… with me.'

Laura, speechless, open-mouthed, so Rosie carried on,
'I told the cops the child was mine, and John, he played along.
Pretended that I'd been with child – I was more rounded then.
Our friends kept quiet and promised silence to the very end.

'We had to change the baby's name and Fred, he was a star.
A brand new birth certificate and, Fred, he has the art.'
'I'm not called Fred The Forge for nowt,' he winked as he explained.
'So Liz had vanished,' Rosie said, 'Now… Laura was her name.'

Rosie paused as Laura stared, amazed at what she'd heard.
This can't be true, some silly joke, it's all just too absurd!
But all their faces, all concerned, convinced her of the tale.
Could it be true, it seems so mad? Yet Rosie was still pale.

'I mean…I don't know…' Laura blustered, 'You're saying, I'm that child?'
Rosie nodded, slowly, softly, eyes bowed all the time.
Laura blinked with tear-filled eyes, composed herself somehow.
'So I must ask, Mum; do you know, where are my parents now?'

**

'Will and Peggy went to ground but, love, I can't say where.
They changed their names, appearance too, their skin tone, noses, hair.
They kept their heads down, played it cool, ne'er threw the cash around.
The cops and gangsters searched for years but never were they found.

'They both enjoyed a carefree life but Will, he took to booze.
He mixed in dodgy company and fights would oft ensue.
In one such fight, poor Will was killed. It happened just last year.
So Peggy chose, now on her own, to come back home… back here.

'She bought a house out in the wilds, a stranger no-one knew,
Except for just a few of us who'd helped her with the move.
She settled in, still very rich although you'd never know,
And married someone that she'd loved so many years ago.

'She'd never truly loved her Will, her heart was set elsewhere.
A man who'd loved her all his life: they'd had a brief affair.
He'd never married, always hoped, he's happy now…eh, Fred?'
Laura, fearful, looked at Pat – 'Mum?' she gently said.

***

'Yes,' said Pat, 'I'm Peggy Rigg and Rosie's sister too.
All that Rosie said to you, I'm sorry, it's all true.
I married Will, I was seduced by promises and lies,
But he was never good for me, I came to realise.'

Laura, still quite overcome, could scarce believe her ears.
Where to start, the hows and whys, the questions, doubts and fears?
So Pat, with Laura at a loss, filled in a few more gaps
And told her of her time abroad and Will, her reckless dad.

'He loved his Liz, his golden girl, up to the stars above.
He left for you, in case he died, a token of his love.
Fred kept in touch. Will had him make your heavy golden ring
With ship engraved – that was his joke, a subtle link to Rigg.'

They talked some more and Laura seemed to take it in her stride.
She understood the secrecy, the necessary lies.
Then all at once, a silence fell, the fire burning low,
And Rosie said, 'There's one more thing, my love, you need to know.'

With worried brow, Pat looked at Laura, then she took her hand.
'What I'm about to tell you, love, I hope you'll understand.
Will and I, we felt such guilt 'bout what we'd done to you.
We planned a safeguard, all of us, Fred, Rosie, me, Bill too.'

'Ah,' said Bill, 'is that my cue?' Pat nodded. 'Okay then.
You might remember, Laura dear, I worked in London town.
Banking was my game back then, all foreign stock and stuff.
A pressure job, a lot at stake, we sometimes played quite rough.

'Well, old Fred here, he got in touch, he asked if I could hold
Some money transferred from abroad, then turn it into gold.
We dealt with ingots all the time so no-one smelt abuse.
Well, Fred's my cousin, as you know, so how could I refuse?

'And bit by bit as time went by, a large amount of cash
Was transformed into bars of gold and hidden in a cache.
Then Fred employed his blacksmith skills and turned the golden bars
Into common household stuff. He really was a star!'

'So where's,' asked Laura, 'all this stuff?' Fred smiled and looked around.
'You're kidding, Fred!' she gasped. 'You mean, it's all here in this house?'
Rosie smiled, 'Oh, yes, my love. It's all been well disguised -
Some pots and pans, the tongs, the urn, the pokers for the fire.'

Laura blinked in wonderment; it must be all a dream.
Her life, her friends, her mum, the house, were never as they seemed.
'And one last thing, love,' Rosie said, 'it may be overdue,
But all the gold stored in this house, my love… it's all for you.'

'That's right,' said Pat. 'Your dad and I, we'd had a golden life
And wanted you to have it too but then was not the time.
And all our friends here, Rosie too, have everything we need.
So, Laura love, it's all for you, to get you on your feet.'

'Before we told you,' Rosie said, 'we wanted to be sure
You'd found a man you would adore, for now and evermore.
We couldn't let the Dagmers get their hands on all our gains,
So Bill and Fred here, and the boys, 'encouraged' Cal away.

'The only other ones who know are Bob and Col and Vince.
Please don't tell Sal, we'll tell her when she grows some common sense.
Well, John, my-ex, Sal's natural dad, of course he knows a tad,
About your parents and the switch but not about the cash.

'So don't discuss it when he calls, he sometimes keeps in touch.
Don't worry, though, he'll never tell, he loves you both too much.'
Pat and Rosie holding hands, now all their cards were played.
What would her reaction be, what would she think and say?

Laura pondered for a while then looked across at Fred,
So many years he'd waited for the girl he was to wed.
And Peggy too, her other mum, a life of ups and downs,
Her daughter always on her mind, the true love that she'd found.

She saw this seasoned loyal gang, how could they be condemned?
She saw the kinship through the years, the bond between true friends.
'I can't pretend I'm not confused,' she said with downcast eyes,
'I'm glad you've told me all the tale and all the hows and whys.

'I thank you all for all you've done, the risks you took for me,
The money, gold, the work you did, I guess not legally?'
Muttered tuts and stifled coughs, 'No harm done…history…
All for the best…don't breathe a word…above board, honestly…'

Laura smiled, 'I understand, your secret's safe with me.
I have a mum, I now have two, how lucky can I be?
So Peggy – Mum – I'll call you Pat forever if I may?'
And Peggy said, 'Of course, my Liz, and you'll stay Laura Hay.'

Then Laura asked, 'So, all this gold, we'll need to change it back
To cash somehow, so we can use it. How do we do that?'
'Well,' said Bill, 'though I'm retired, I still have certain skills.
A phone call here, a phone call there, your coffer will be filled!'

Rosie smiled, was so relieved that things had turned out well,
That Laura was set up for life and Christmas wedding bells.
'I think,' she said, 'some fine Champagne, or else a cup of tea?'
'Thanks,' said Fred, 'I'll have a glass.' 'And me!' 'And me!' 'And me!'

The hope that weddings bring

T'was Christmas Eve; the icy clouds had scurried far away.
The sun was bright, the air was sharp, it was a bonny day.
The morning frost had thawed away, dewed webs bedecked the grass.
Robins danced through holly trees, crisp leaves adorned the paths.

An eager crowd had gathered round the gate to Porlock church,
All dressed in finest suits and frocks, grand hats and classic shirts.
The Christmas lights enwrapped the trees with stars atop of gold.
Carols drifted from the porch to warm their Yuletide souls.

One by one from out the pub, the old boys slowly lurched
Towards their mostly patient wives who waited by the church.
Just in time to hear, then see, the tractor rumbling down
From up the hill, with Laura in her silken wedding gown.

The ladies gasped to see the bride, so beautiful and fair,
So graceful in her glowing white and flowers in her hair.
The crowd went in as Laura waited, tried a nervous smile.
Fred kissed her cheek then took her hand and led her up the aisle.

***

Then, up the moor to Jack's old barn; everyone was there
To party with the finest ale and best of Exmoor fare.
All their friends, their kith and kin and distant cousins too
Came to toast the happy pair, rejoice in love so true.

Laura had told all to Jack, the full uncensored tale.
The secret was secure, he vowed, unto his dying day.
Cal sent down, ten years in gaol for drugs and other crimes,
Wounding, threats, illegal brews; Mog, eighteen months plus fines.

Now recovered, bridesmaid Sal admitted her mistakes;
She'd mixed with villains, been a fool, poor judgements that she'd made.
Laughing, hugging, hand in hand, she danced all through the night
With sunny Spider, Jack's best man; 'He has a cheeky smile!' .

A lull amidst the revelry, another DJ break.
Jack and Laura, hand in hand and smiling, took the stage.
'A bit of quiet, please, everyone,' Jack said, 'We have some news.
The farm has done quite well this year, we have some savings too.

'The Dagmer farm is up for sale now Cal has gone to gaol.
We put a bid in just last week – today agreed the sale!'
Cheers and whistles all around, congrats and drunken hugs.
The dancefloor heaved to celebrate the happy times to come.

An evening made for love and joy, the hope that weddings bring.
Pete The Prowl was hopeful too – he checked for wedding rings.
Jack and Laura took a break, a rest 'midst all the din.
They strolled outside to take some air and met a tipsy Vince.

Some cheerful chat and more congrats, then Laura quietly asked,
'You've helped us out so much, so thanks, but why all this for us?'
Vince looked askance and took a sip. 'Well, Will was my close friend.
I was a cop when Will and Peggy pulled their stunt and went.

'I can't condone what Will had done but I admired his balls.
Escape scot-free with gangster loot, well, who'd believe it all?
I knew they'd left you with your aunt, all for the best of course.
I lost my drive soon after that, resigned and left the force.'

'Since then, I've helped as best I could, for you and Rosie too,
And, with the boys, have watched your backs in case things went askew.
To me, they're like my family, we've been through thick and thin.
Ah, here they are now! Come here, boys – come and join the team!'

With half-filled drinks, a swaying group escaped the rowdy barn.
Bob and Col and Bill and Fred. 'Great news about the farm!
Phase Two complete!' Bill winked to Jack, 'Successful transfer too.'
They'd all had fun, a great result, a most successful coup!

Laura thanked them. Bill replied, 'Just glad to help, my dear.
I mean, we're all your family, that's what we do round here.
Fred's my cousin, so is Bob, and Col, he is a Hay.
We stick together, come what may, that is the Exmoor way.'

Then Bill disclosed he'd heard from Bo; a disappointing turn –
Now not related to a lord or peers from Ashley Combe.
His forebear was a butler there for many years, that's all.
Bo said he'd come back sometime soon, he'd really had a ball!

Reliving all their derring-do, the exploits and affrays,
They wouldn't tell a living soul until their dying day.
And then Vince paused and looked quite doleful, then he reminisced,
'I really wish that Bo was here, he was a part of this.'

They chatted on, and then a whooping from the track below.
From out the darkness, James appeared and with him, smiling… Bo.
'Just got here, guys, my plane was late. It's great to see you here!
I wouldn't miss this for the world. I'll get you all a beer!'

Other tales from Exmoor

The Porlock Smuggler's Tale

We knows each cave and hidden dell along the Porlock coast.
By night we go, we land the loads; the brandy pays the most.
The bearers come and move them on, no lights, no duty paid.
Some gold in hand, our shady band are merchants of free trade.

In Spring this year, old Excise Jim was gaoled for taking bribes,
And new man Jack is hard to crack, he's keen, has watchful eyes.
A godly man of simple needs, he's ardent in his checks.
So we pretend to be good lads 'cos, truth, we like our necks.

That time, that wine, remember that? From Portugal or Spain.
The bottles hid in walls and floors, in straw, you know the game.
Then Jack strode in and found the lot. I offered him a swig.
'No chance', he says, 'Can't stand the stuff. Like all this wine, you're nicked!'

I tries me best to earn a crust, to move whatever sells.
No luck this time, a rueful smile, a night locked in the cells.

When rum came in, the moon was bright, we spun a spectral tale.
A funeral of ghosts; if seen, would kill you without fail.
Most stayed at home, except for Jack who caught us by the Weir.
Betrayed by Spot, our windy nag, or bottle-clanking bier.

Our cart was broke when sacks of tea came in one rainy dawn.
So, putting on our wives' full frocks, we stuffed them down our drawers.
All went well 'til Excise Jack saw make-up washed away,
And stubble on one pouting maid. Back to the clink again.

I tries me best to earn a crust, to move whatever sells.
No luck this time, a rueful smile, two nights locked in the cells.

Our favourite load, a brandy boat, ten barrels in from France.
To check the strength, we poured a cup – it's wise to take no chance.
But Spot drank some and kicked the cart. Jack heard, came at a run.
Our bribes no good – that tiresome man hates brandy, tea and rum.

Some crates of leaves to put in pipes came in one wintry night.
We smoked some in our Culbone cave, our heads felt very light.
I think the smoke gave us away, this time not Jack's keen men,
But honest traders with a grudge; we grabbed the stash and fled.

So with our gold we laugh and joke, return to Porlock town,
And spend all night, our heads still light, in The Ship or Rose And Crown.

December nights, dark ships sail in to catch the Christmas trade,
To Bristol docks, fine silks and lace in florid fragrant crates.
Some come our way but, sure enough, that Jack is on our heels.
He's caught us – but he then suggests a most surprising deal.

'Times are rather hard,' he says, 'and Yuletide's nearly here.
My wife likes all those fancy clothes but they are far too dear.
To keep her sweet, could you slip me some silks in silvered grey?
Then, when I spots your smuggling ways, I'll look the other way.'

The cider flows, the friendships grow, our Jack's now one of us.
We raise a jar to better times, free trade and those we trust.

The Saga of St Dubricius

As history tells, when Romans left, the Saxons came in hordes,
And noble Arthur, king of all, fought back with spear and sword.
He had as friend a bishop wise, old Dyfrig of Caerleon,
A fearless man with heart of gold and faith as strong as iron.

One day Dyfrig was in Llantwit, a coastal seat in Wales,
When sudden clamour broke the peace, fast hooves and clank of mail.
A breathless horseman skidded in with word from Badon Hill,
Where Arthur faced the Saxon foe; this fight would test their skill.

The news was that the enemy had called for further aid;
A fleet of Saxon ships approached, just several hours away.
A plea from Arthur to his friend – Dyfrig must head them off.
Use whatever means he had: the Saxons must be stopped!

Dyfrig looked out across the sea and, sure enough, he saw
Ten mighty ships; the sunlight gleamed on spears prepared for war.
What could he do? All Arthur's men were occupied elsewhere.
Could farmers stop this Saxon fleet with forks and mere plough-shares?

He knew the tide was strong that day but would it be enough?
The ships came on, their fearsome load was made of sterner stuff.
A shadow passed across the sun, a sign of portents grave.
Dyfrig felt helpless in his plight, so he knelt down and prayed.

Now, at this time a giant ruled the hills of northern Wales,
A vicious brute who conquered kings and terrorized the vales.
His name was Rhitta and he loved to cut from vanquished foes
Their beards, to fashion rugged coats, new hats and hairy clothes.

The only king he hadn't quelled was Arthur so he strode
Towards the sea and Camelot, the British king's abode.
Unaware that Arthur was away from home for days,
He paused to ford the Channel at a shallow crossing place.

By chance, he'd stopped where Dyfrig prayed, wrapped in his humble shroud.
The bishop saw the shadow move, too fast for passing cloud.
He turned his head and saw the giant and, shocked, fell on his back,
But Rhitta heard the noise and looked, and thought 'Mm, tasty snack!'

But Dyfrig was a sturdy soul so stood up, waved his staff.
Undaunted by this monstrous man that blocked his exit path.
As Rhitta reached down for his meal, Dyfrig was fleet of mind
And shrewdly planned a crafty ruse, before the giant could dine.

'Pray, stop!' he yelled, 'Just look at me, a scrawny wizened wretch.
Why munch on me when, out at sea, young blood is yours to catch?
Just look out there, four hundred men, and all with beards so black.
I bet they taste good and their hair would make a lovely hat.'

As Dyfrig pointed, Rhitta looked and saw the Saxon fleet
Approaching fast but far away; he couldn't miss this treat.
He ran into the frothy waves, ignoring Dyfrig there.
It would be lovely, for a change, to try some foreign fare.

The Saxon troops then saw the threat and veered to southern shore,
The sails were up, the tide was strong, tight muscles strained on oars.
But Rhitta was too quick for them, and with a mighty bound
Engulfed the ships; the splash was heard for many miles around.

The wave was huge; the seabed rocks were thrust towards the land
And formed a mighty pebble ridge that covered all the sand.
The Saxon ships were all but smashed, except for only two,
That Rhitta's outstretched arms had missed; they were the lucky few.

Towards the coast these ships were hurled, on racing crest of wave.
One came to rest, all dashed and torn, beside the crescent bay.
The other ship went further still, was washed on up a hill
And rested near a village square; some bits remain there still.

Down in the sea, the hungry giant caught men on every side.
But Rhitta, belly far from full, forgot the vicious tide.
He overstepped and slipped and flailed, recovered, but too late.
The surge swept Rhitta off his feet, to deep sea and his fate.

The story spread across the land of Dyfrig's epic feat.
This man of God had conquered fiends, a holy soul indeed.
He was declared a modern saint, Dubricius his new name.
A church was built in old Porlock, the place above the bay.

And where the Saxon ships lay torn, wood smashed and mainsails ripped,
Two pubs were built and aptly named the Top and Bottom Ships.
Unto this day are glasses raised to bishop Dyfrig's health,
To keeping evil from our shores, to freedom, love and wealth.

The Legend of Old Black Paw

The creatures of the moor were scared, they all stayed home at night.
A Beast, they said, would roam and prey when darkness hid the floor.
Some say they've seen it, heard it, smelled it. None would dare to fight
The devil from the depths of Hell – they called it Old Black Paw.

Its lair was in the darkest woods where none would ever go,
In shadow of a lonesome crag, 'neath oak or holly tree.
The ground, they said, was carpeted with fur and shattered bones
Of voles for breakfast, mice for lunch and fattened dogs for tea.

Now once upon a summer time, a brave new dog turned up.
A sniffer with a first class nose, a smart and fearless pooch.
His name was Bay, a Master Hound, a hero since a pup,
But slower now, being five years old and over fond of food.

He loved the moor and soon he knew all paths and rabbit runs,
Met birds and bats and mice and rats, knew most of them by name.
But saw that as the sun went down they vanished, every one,
In fear of Paw. Bay saw a chance to win heroic fame.

That summer was a glorious one and Bay searched high and low
For Old Black Paw but found no trace in ditch nor bush nor hole.
He asked the bees, the jays, the sheep, he sniffed each thick hedgerow,
Ran panting through the gorse and grass, asked every worm and mole.

The land was dry as solid rock and Bay's famed nose worked hard.
A fruitless search in scorching sun so he lay down to rest.
The butterflies and sparrows played their chase games near and far,
And Bay stretched out to go to sleep beneath a chaffinch nest.

A rumble in the blackened sky, a wind then drops of rain,
So Bay ran off towards the trees as floods drenched earth and stone.
The storm soon passed but, dripping there, Bay caught a scent untamed,
A dangerous, wild, exotic smell, the strangest that he'd known.

With hackles high, he tiptoed on into the shadowed woods.
A startled blackbird's echoed call, then silence chilled his soul.
Now tangled trees and dead brown leaves from winter's deadly hood.
In land unknown beneath an oak, Bay found a huge black hole.

He peered and saw the glow of eyes, the glint of sharpened teeth,
A massive face with fur-set jowls. It roared! It meant him harm.
Its form crept out as Bay shrank back, it loomed o'er Bay beneath.
With razor claws and dripping maw and bigger than a barn.

It leapt. Bay squeaked and closed his eyes, he knew his end had come.
But then heard, 'Got him!' from behind. He turned around, amazed.
'What's that?' asked Bay in trembling voice. 'A wasp', said Beast. 'Just one.
They're nesting in that tree up there, been bugging me for days.'

The Beast sat down and Bay relaxed and dared to ask its tale.
'I'm just a cat,' Old BP said. 'I've never known my mum.
They left me in the woods one day, not far from this old trail.
I cried and wailed and crept and hid. I've never had much fun.

'I think I've eaten far too much as now I'm rather huge.
The other creatures all seem scared, they always stay away.
I'm not a monster, just a cat. My name is Dusky Su.
I just want friends and warmth and care, and fresh milk every day.'

Promising to be back soon, Bay wandered homeward bound.
He yearned to be a Master Friend, help Su as best he can.
Next day, he gathered all his friends, spoke of the cat he'd found.
They talked and talked and soon they had a very cunning plan.

He sought out Su and sat her down. 'We'll get you small,' he said.
'Lots of games and much less food. Play hide-and-seek with wrens.
Chase the fastest squirrels round the trees before your bed.
And don't eat rabbits (too much fat) then they can be your friends.'

She loved the plan and soon the two would daily exercise.
Bay got so thin, his little legs could scarce keep up with Su.
To hide the plan from human eyes, disguise his change of size,
Bay ate and ate to put on weight, the noble thing to do.

The other creatures of the Moor helped Su in every way.
They knew the fear of Old Black Paw would soon be gone for good.
The rabbits made a bramble stew for Su's tea every day,
The chickens and the ducks gave eggs and corn soup for her pud.

The fastest squirrels loved the chase, Su loved the games they played.
Up and down the trees they ran, the boughs were torn and bent.
She sheltered in the badgers' setts from rain as she lost weight.
The foxes lured bad dogs away from Su's exotic scent.

72

The hawks were generals in the sky, sharp-eyed for every risk.
The humans mustn't know of Su! The owls kept watch at night.
The bats were guards of walkers' paths, awakening at dusk.
They weaved and squeaked and swooped and spun and zipped in jagged flight.

A few weeks passed – the plan had worked and Su was small again.
A happy cat, no more a Beast, pals won and huge size lost.
She partied in the evening woods with Bay and all her friends.
The spiders joined in cheerfully and feasted on the wasps.

Along the village path Su strode before the sun came up.
Back to warmth and milk and love. Her story ends with that.
To celebrate, Bay had to eat, so sneaked into The Ship.
A crafty Master Sausage Thief, he gorged himself 'til fat.

He ate and ate as well deserved a Hero Hound so wise.
But guilt and shame at barrelled tum made fat Bay slink away.
He stayed in Su's den, far away from light and prying eyes
And ate 'til huge, a monstrous dog,

A tale for another day…

Printed in Great Britain
by Amazon